EARLY AMERICAN CRAFTS AND TRADES

EDITED, WITH A NEW INTRODUCTION, BY

Peter Stockham

DOVER PUBLICATIONS, INC.

NEW YORK

This Dover edition, first published in 1976 as *Little Book of Early American Crafts and Trades*, is an unabridged republication of Part I of the work as published by Jacob Johnson in Whitehall (Philadelphia) and Richmond in 1807 under the title *The Book of Trades, or Library of the Useful Arts*. A new Introduction has been written by Peter Stockham especially for the Dover edition.

International Standard Book Number: 0-486-23336-7
Library of Congress Catalog Card Number: 75-46194

Manufactured in the United States of America
Dover Publications, Inc.
31 East 2nd Street
Mineola, N.Y. 11501

Introduction
to the Dover Edition

This is one of the earliest nineteenth-century books of trades for children, but the tradition for such books goes back a long way to the early days of printing. Those who have seen the illustrations for trades in Jost Amman's and Hans Sachs' *Book of Trades* (1568, also reprinted by Dover Publications) will easily recognize the similarity of many of the illustrations in the book reproduced here, *Early American Crafts and Trades* (original title: *The Book of Trades, or Library of the Useful Arts*). Things had not changed much in the intervening years, and this is particularly true of the trades which we now call crafts. Works such as Comenius's *Orbis Pictus* (first published in 1654 and in many editions up to the present time) concentrate on the arts and crafts, and Hoole in his famous edition of Comenius of 1659 mentions that he intended the work to interest children of six or seven. Although schoolbooks for children have existed for hundreds of years, books of entertainment (albeit often with didactic overtones) do not appear until the mid-eighteenth century, and it is this combination of entertainment with instruction that one finds in this book of trades.

The book we reproduce has an interesting, but complex, bibliographical history. It was first published in England in 1804 by Tabart & Company, but this American first edition (published by Jacob Johnson "and for sale at his book-stores in Philadelphia and in Richmond, Virginia") was copied from the third edition of 1806, where the number of copperplates had been increased from the 18 of the first edition to the 23 of the present edition. The copperplates were copied from the English edition and in some cases were reversed in printing, with the result that it is necessary to read "right" for "left" in the text, and vice versa; in other cases the engraver reproduced the engraving correctly, and for these, text references are accurate as given. Over a period of time the text was revised, and because the work was very popular during the first half of the nineteenth century there are numerous different editions. No copyright appears to have subsisted in the work, and in fact there was one year in which two different editions of the work were published, with two different updatings, from two separate publishers, the basis being the original Tabart edition of 1804.

By 1825 it had been necessary to add a supplement "of machines," and the increasingly complex nature of industrial trades is reflected in later books of trades down to the end of the nineteenth century. All of these editions must have encouraged many young people to think of their future careers.

Surprisingly there is no introduction to this work either in its British or American editions, but other similar works of the period stress the intention "to acquaint the rising generation with our various trades and their origin and history," and a later edition of this present work (London, R. Phillips, 1821) says "in a commercial empire, like the United Kingdom, to acquaint the rising generation with details of various trades, and with their origin and history, must be considered a praiseworthy effort." "All knowledge and wonder (which is the seed of knowledge) is an impression of pleasure in itself"—this saying of Francis Bacon was still very much an influence on the pre-Victorian compilers of this kind of work, a tradition which continued through early Victorian times. Even if we find a more developed workshop or small factory in some of the illustrations, there is still the feeling that a finished product is being produced by individual effort rather than by the developed factory-bench system of later industry. Several books of trades as late as the 1880's were still showing many illustrations which differed little in detail from these early illustrations. It is true, of course, that by the 1880's many of the processes had been broken down in the larger industries, and the most immediate impression of these early plates from 1807 is of individual enterprise.

An early contemporary review of the British edition of this work (and the two parts which originally followed it) by the indefatigable Mrs. Trimmer (from her *Guardian of Education*, Vol. IV, 1805) makes interesting reading:

> ART. v.—*The Book of Trades; or, Library of the Useful Arts. In Three Parts. Illustrated with Copper Plates.* Price 3s. 6d. each Number, plain; or 5s. with the Plates coloured: either Part to be had separately. Tabart and Co. 1805.
>
> This is a very amusing and instructive work, from which a general idea of a number of useful arts carried on in this and other kingdoms, may be gained. Subjects of this kind are very proper for young minds to be occupied with in their hours of amusement, when they are not proposed in too scientific a way; an objection which cannot be made to any that are introduced in these volumes. The plates in the three Numbers amount to 59, each of which exhibits a manufacturer with his machinery about him, and in such a manner as, with the aid of the description, to give a lively idea of what he is about. A few of the Prints relate to the employments of women, namely, the Straw-Hat-maker, the Lace-maker; the Milliner; the Feather-worker; the Laundress. These we think, in general, frivolous, excepting that the Prints are pretty. We recommend this Book

> as a valuable acquisition to the Juvenile Library. The Plates are uncommonly good.

The substance of these books of trades has to be imagined against the background of a reader of the time, who probably lived in a village or small town, in a community which was largely self-sufficient, and who would be familiar with many of the practitioners of these trades, however we may think of them as being highly specialized and having little local demand. Each community would have its local craft workshops; and many domestic crafts such as brewing, lacemaking, and dressmaking were widely practiced. Many farm products were processed by local mills, and in their turn could be used locally by the craftsman; these books illustrate already, however, the movement of finished products from one area to another (often by means of trade fairs, but also by exchange of finished goods for further supplies of raw material for manufacture), and the breaking down of the purely self-sufficient community of a hundred years earlier. The local craftsman would still satisfy local needs for tools, for services such as printing, and for items of everyday use and wear, such as shoes and saddles.

The end of the eighteenth century and the beginning of the nineteenth saw a great increase in the application of invention to solving problems previously not thought worth solving, and this meant a shift from the simple tooled craftsman to the man who used a machine to solve many of his problems. An example of this can be seen under the entry on the Spinner on page 12, where the inventions of Richard Arkwright are mentioned. But often these machines were very simple indeed. The machine used by the straw-hat maker to split the straw plait is an example (see page 111). Foreign competition induced the British straw industry to start splitting straws only in about 1800, and this fairly recent innovation is mentioned in this book of trades.

Some trades could not be supported by the comparatively small local communities, and this led to the practice of journeymen traveling around an area. The cooper (page 56) carried with him a few different-sized hoops and provided a varied and reasonably widespread service satisfying a variety of local needs. Many of the workers in these trades were paid on a piece-rate basis, and this book contains many interesting details of the methods of payment and the rates for different jobs. It is possible from this information to make guesses both as to the social status of different trades, and also the skills of the individuals practicing them. Some of the trades, regarded as highly specialized, still had a controlled system of entry; this, of course, implied that those entering them could command greater rewards for their services. Persons serving an apprenticeship to an apothecary, for example (see page 102), were bound for eight years.

Nowadays books such as these seem almost do-it-yourself manuals, and it is tempting to try and see if, with the simple tools and materials required, it would be possible for us actually to do some of the trades. Certainly some are described with great knowledge and understanding of how they were done. Others, however, are not accurately described, and the drawings lack a vital detail or two. Later editions attempt to improve on the details, broaden the picture by expanding the marketing and manufacturing details, and show how the trades developed, some quite quickly, through the early years of the nineteenth century.

William Darton, writing in a similar *Little Jack of All Trades* (1804, 1806), remarks, "Until very lately, children's books were allowed coarse wooden cuts: but now the copperplate engraver condescends to work for them also; and, you must allow, the pictures adorning this work are a very pleasing specimen of his art." Readers of this present reprint, which can be read and looked at with many different interests in mind, will, I am sure, agree.

PETER STOCKHAM

London, October, 1975

CONTENTS

*** There is a Plate to each Trade.

A Wool Comber.

THE WOOL-COMBER.

THE attitude of the wool-comber, in the plate, exhibits him in only one part of his business, the drawing out of the slivers. The wool upon which he works, is the hair or covering of the sheep, which when washed, and combed, and spun, and woven, makes worsted, many kinds of stuff, and other articles of great use in the concerns of life.

While the wool remains in the state in which it is shorn from the sheep's back, it is called a fleece. Each fleece consists of wool of different qualities and degrees of fineness, which the wool-stapler sorts, and sells at different rates. The finest wool grows on and about the head of the sheep, and the coarsest about the tail. The shortest is on the head and some parts of the belly, the longest on the flanks.

Wool is either shorn, or pulled off the skin after the sheep is dead : in the first case it is called *fleece*-wool : the other sort, called *skin*-wool, if very short, is used much in the manufacture of hats.

The wool intended for the manufacture of stuffs is brought into a state adapted for the making of worsted by the wool-comber. He first washes the wool in a trough, and, when very clean, puts one end on a fixed hook, and the other on a moveable hook, which he turns round with a handle, till all the moisture be drained completely out. It is then thrown lightly out into a basket, such as is seen in the plate. The wool-comber next throws it out into thin layers, on each of which he scatters a few drops of oil ; it is then put together closely into a bin, which is placed under the bench on which he sits : at the back of the wool-bin is another and larger one for the *noyles,* that is, the part of the wool that is left on the comb after the sliver is drawn out.

The shape of the comb is seen in the plate : there are in each comb three rows of teeth parallel to one another. The best combs are manufactured at Halifax in Yorkshire : the teeth are made of highly tempered steel, and fixed into a very smooth stock, in which is inserted a handle nearly in a perpendicular position. Each workman has two of these combs : these he makes pretty hot, by putting them into a sort of jar made of clay, *(see the plate)* called a comb-pot, in which there is' a fire made of the best burnt charcoal.

When the combs are hot, he puts on

each a certain quantity of wool, having first disentangled it from all knots, and other obstacles that might impede the operation. He then combs the wool from off one comb on to the other alternately, till it is exceedingly smooth; when having again heated the combs, he fixes each on an iron spike placed in the wall for the purpose, as it is represented in the plate, and draws out the wool into a fine sliver, oftentimes five or six feet in length: what is left on the comb is called a noyle, and is fit only for the manufacture of blankets and coarse cloth.

In general, four wool-combers work at the same pot, which is made large enough to admit of eight combs. There are, of course, four distinct benches and bins of both kinds in each shop. In almost every workshop is an hour-glass, by which they measure the time: the care of this falls to the lot of a particular person.

The small bottle underneath the comb is filled with oil, which is occasionally used. On the side of the wall are placed two ballads, of which, in general, there are several in every wool-comber's shop.

The journeymen work by the piece, and will earn from sixteen shillings to twenty per week. Like people in many other trades, they often make holidays in the early part of the week. They come on a Monday morning, and, having lighted the fire in the comb-pot, will frequently go away, and perhaps return no more till Wednesday or even Thursday. The men in this trade have a curious custom : when out of work, they set out in search of a master, with a sort of certificate from their last place; this they call going on the *tramp;* and at every shop where they call, and can get no employment, they receive one penny, which is given from a common stock raised by the men of that shop.   A spare bench is always provided in the shop, upon which people on the *tramp* may rest themselves.

Wool combing is preparatory to the manufacture of worsted yarn, and is the first process towards the making of flannels, serges, stuffs, baize, kerseys, &c.

The invention of wool-combing is ascribed to bishop Blaize, the patron saint of the trade, in honour of whom, a splendid festival is annually kept by the whole body of wool-combers in this kingdom on the third of February.

The woolen manufactory makes a principal article in our foreign and domestic trade.

A pack of wool weighs 240lbs. and, it is said, will employ more than sixty persons a week to manufacture it into cloths, viz. three men to sort, dry, mix, and make it ready for the carder; five to scribble it; thirty-five women and girls to card and spin it; eight men to weave it; four to spole it; and eight to scour, mill, pack, and press it.

When the wool is made into stuffs, serges, &c., it will employ 200 persons. And when made into stockings it will afford work for a week to 184 persons, viz. 10 combers, 102 spinners, winders, &c., and 60 stocking-weavers, besides doublers, throwers, and a dyer.

THE SPINNER.

IN many country villages the art of spinning is carried on by women and children in the open air, as it is represented in the plate. Spinning is applied to the reducing of silk, flax, hemp, wool, hair, &c., into thread.

Spinning by hand is performed either
with the distaff and spindle, or on the
wheel: in the former case the person sits
to her work; in the latter she stands, or
rather runs backwards and forwards.
We shall describe both methods. When
the distaff and spindle are used, the flax
or other substance is tied or fixed on
a long stick: the spinner draws out a
thread, which she fixes to her spindle;
then with her left hand she turns the
wheel, and with her right guides the
thread drawn from the flax, &c. round
the spindle, or rather round a spole which
goes on the spindle. When a sufficient
quantity is wound on the spole, it is
taken off, thrown into the basket, and
replaced by an empty one.

Spinning of wool is managed by a different process. Here the wool, in those
fine slivers taken from the wool-comber,
is held in the hand; a thread of it is fast-

Spinner.

WR sc.

ened to the wheel, which the spinner turns with velocity, and runs backward from it, thereby drawing out the thread to a considerable length. In either mode of spinning, when the spindle is filled, its thread is wound upon a reel, and taken off in the form of a skain or hank. The wool is delivered out to the spinner by weight, and when she returns it it is again weighed. Women must be very expert who can earn at this business one shilling in a day. Children at an early age are taught the art, and will soon earn from six-pence to one and six-pence a week.

Besides the above mode of spinning wool upon the wheel, a more antient method is still practised in the county of Norfolk, with the distaff and spindle, which may be used either sitting, or walking while the spinner tends on cows, poultry, &c. The sliver of wool is braid-

ed round the distaff (or *rock* as it is called
by the Norfolk spinners), from the slit
end of which a thread is drawn and fastened to the slender spindle, which receives a whirling motion by being quickly rolled upon a piece of smooth leather
called the trip-skin, fastened upon the
thigh of the spinner, who with one hand
gently draws a few hairs from the tail of
the sliver, while the other winds up the
spindle and renews its whirling motion.
In this way finer yarn is made than by
any other method, but more than six-
pence per day can seldom be earned.

Spinners are employed by the master
wool-combers, the whole of whose trade
may be properly described in this article.
The act of combing the wool has been
already noticed. Spinning the wool into
skains is the next process : these are
afterwards put into the hands of other
women, called *winders,* whose business

is, by means of a wheel and other simple apparatus, to wind two, three, or more of these skains together, so as to make a compound thread of them. This thread is wound on to spoles or bobbins, for the convenience of having them fixed on spindles, which are turned round by mill-work in order to twist the threads thus combined into a firm substance. When taken from the mill, the worsted is washed, dyed, and dried; it is then done up in crewels, and fit for sale.

The business of the wool-comber is different in different countries: some, as the wool-combers in Hertfordshire, prepare it only for worsted yarn, &c. others, as those in and near Norwich, prepare it for weaving into camblets and other light stuffs.

Sometimes the worsted is required to be very white: in that case, before it is dry, after washing, it is hung up in a

close room, in which a charcoal fire is
burning : on the fire some finely pow-
dered roll-brimstone is thrown, and the
room made air-tight, so as neither to admit the external air, nor suffer the vapour
from the sulphur to escape.

The variety and importance of those
branches of our manufactures which are
produced from cotton, wool, flax, spun
into yarn, have occasioned many at-
tempts to render spinning more easy,
cheap, and expeditious, by means of
complicated machinery Several of these
have been very successful ; particularly
those for cotton by Sir Richard Arkwright ; but the spinning-mill has not as
yet been able to afford worsted yarn so
cheap as that which is spun by hand.

The art of spinning is not confined
to the human race ; it is given to many
animals for their preservation, and for
other purposes. Spiders, caterpillars, &c.

make threads of any length that they please, by forcing the viscous liquor of which they are formed, through a fine perforation in the organ appointed for this spinning. This art is even extended to the inhabitants of the sea. The muscle possesses it in a great degree of perfection. But the method adopted by this shell-fish is very different from that made use of by caterpillars and silkworms. The latter in their work resemble the business of the wire-drawer; the former, that of the founder, who casts his metal in a mould. The canal of the organ destined for the muscle's spinning, which is called its tongue, is the mould in which the thread is cast.

THE WATERMAN.

WATERMEN are such as row in boats, and ply for fares on the river Thames. Their business probably originated from necessity. Before the bridges were erected, the intercourse which must necessarily be carried on by persons on both sides of the Thames would strike out employment for a number of people who should undertake to convey persons and luggage from London and Westminster to Southwark, Lambeth, &c. London-bridge is of great antiquity; but Westminster-bridge has not been finished much more than half a century, and the bridge at Blackfriars was not completed till the year 1769.

A waterman requires but little to enable him to begin business, viz. a boat, a pair of oars, and a long pole with an iron point and hook at the lower end,

Waterman.

the whole cost of which is not more than twenty pounds.

Sometimes two men belong to one boat; in other cases, a boat belongs to a single waterman. In the former, it is called *oars;* in the latter, it is called a *sculler;* and at the water-side, when they ply for fare, the cry is " *Oars, sir,*" " *Sculler, sir,*" according as the boat is rowed by two men, or by a single man.

The boat, and indeed the whole business of a waterman, are regulated by divers acts of parliament. The names of the men who ply for fares are registered, and their boats numbered; they must be twelve feet and a half long, and four feet and a half broad; and if any are found under this size they are liable to be forfeited.

No persons are allowed to ply on the river but such as have been apprentices to watermen seven years; or are, at the time, apprentices, and have worked with some able watermen at least two years, and are sixteen years of age.

Besides benches for the watermen, there is good accommodation for five or six persons, in the common wherry-boats.

The oars are long pieces of timber scooped out into a thin slice at one end, and round or square at the other. That part of the oar which is out of the vessel, and which enters the water, is called the blade ; the other is called the loom, the extremity of which, being small enough to be grasped by the hand, is called the handle.   The place in which the oar rests is called the *row-lock.*

When there are two or more water-men in the same boat, their oars move in perfect unison ; to which Shakespeare refers in his Anthony and Cleopatra :

. . . . : . The oars were silver,
Which to the tune of flutes kept stroke, and made
The water which they beat, to follow faster.

The use of the pole is to push off a
boat from land. The waterman in the
plate is represented as using it for that
purpose; and the hook enables him to
draw his boat to shore, or close to another
boat. The post and ring in the fore
ground of the plate are intended to moor
the boats to, when they are not wanted.
At night a chain is passed through the
ring, and the whole is rendered secure
by means of a padlock.

The oval figure on the waterman's
arm represents a silver badge which he
has gained by his dexterity in rowing.
Thomas Dogget, who was zealously
attached to the house of Hanover, left
by his will a sum of money to provide a
coat and silver badge, which are to be

rowed for, from London-bridge to Chelsea, by six watermen annually on the
first of August, the day on which George
the first ascended the throne of these
realms.   To the person who carries off
the prize there are certain other privi-
leges attached; one of which is, that he
cannot, like other watermen, be pressed
into his majesty's sea service. The fares
of watermen are regulated by the lord
mayor and aldermen, who are invested
with full authority to hear and deter-
mine all complaints of acts of misbe-
haviour.

Tilt-boats, which are used for con-
veying passengers and luggage between
London-bridge and Gravesend, are subject to strict regulations, as well as the
common wherry-boats. Tilt-boats must
be of fifteen tons burthen; and two officers are appointed, one at Billingsgate
and the other at Gravesend, to ring a

bell for the tilt-boats to put off; and those which do not proceed with two sufficient men, within fifteen minutes after the ringing of the bell, are subject to a penalty of five pounds.

If any waterman between Gravesend and Windsor receive into his boat or barge a greater number of persons than the act allows, and a passenger happen to be drowned, such waterman is deemed guilty of felony, and liable to transportation.

THE BASKET-MAKER.

BASKETS are made of willows, which according to their manner of growth are called osiers and sallows. They thrive best in moist places; and the proprietors of such marsh lands generally let what they call the willow-beds to persons who cut them at certain seasons, and prepare them for basket-makers. To form an osier-bed, the land should be divided into plots six, eight, or ten feet broad, by narrow ditches; and if there is a power of keeping water in these cuts at pleasure, by means of a sluice, it is highly advantageous in many seasons. Osiers planted in small spots, and along hedges, will supply a farmer with hurdle-stuff, as well as with a profusion of all sorts of baskets. The common osier is cut at three years, but that with yellow bark is permitted to remain a year longer.

When the osiers are cut down, those that are intended for white work, such as baskets used in washing, are to be stripped of their bark or rinds while green. This is done by means of a sharp instrument, fixed into a firm block: the osiers are passed over this, and stripped of their covering with great velocity.

A Basket-maker.

They are then dried, and put in bundles
for sale. Before they are worked up,
they must be previously soaked in water,
which gives them flexibility. The mode
of operation is very well displayed in
the print : the basket-maker usually sits
on the ground to his business, unless
when the baskets are too large for him
to reach their upper parts in that position.

Hampers and other coarse work are
made of osiers without any previous preparation except soaking. It requires no
great capital either of money or ingenuity to exercise the business of a basket-
maker. Some expert workmen make a
variety of articles of wicker manufacture,
as work-baskets of different descriptions.
Even in the coarser articles, a man well
skilled in his trade will earn three or
four shillings a day. On the right and
left of the plate we see bundles of osiers

ready for use; on the ground by the side of the workman there are some with which he is at work; and round about him are a variety of different kinds of baskets upon which he has shown his skill.

By some accident it once happened that a rich man and a poor pennyless basket-maker were thrown on a distant island, inhabited only by a savage race of men. The former seeing himself exposed to apparent danger, without the means of assistance or defence, and ignorant of the language of the people in whose power he was, began to cry and wring his hands in a piteous manner: but the poor man, ever accustomed to labour, made signs to the people, that he was desirous of becoming useful to them; on which account they treated him with kindness, but the other they regarded with contempt.

One of the savages found something
like a fillet, with which he adorned his
forehead, and seemed to think himself
exremely fine. The basket-maker, taking advantage of his vanity, pulled up
some reeds, and, sitting down to work,
in a short time finished a very elegant
wreath, which he placed upon the head
of the first inhabitant he chanced to meet.
This man was so pleased with his new
acquisition, that he danced and capered
about for joy, and ran to seek his com-
panions, who were all struck with asto-
nishment at this new and elegant piece
of finery. It was not long before another came to the basket-maker, making
signs that he also wanted to be ornamented like his companion ; and with
such pleasure were these chaplets received by the whole tribe, that the basket-maker was continually employed in
weaving them. In return for the plea-

sure which he conferred upon them, the grateful savages brought him every kind of food which their country afforded, built him a hut, and showed him every demonstration of gratitude and kindness. But the rich man, who possessed neither talents to please, nor strength to labour, was condemned to be the basket-maker's servant, and to cut him reeds to supply the continual demand for chaplets.— Such are the advantages of industry and ingenuity.

On the shores of North America is found a remarkable fish called the BASKET-fish. Its body resembles that of a star-fish, and it is furnished with numerouse arms to catch its prey. When caught with a hook, it clasps the bait, and encircles it with its many arms coming up in the form of a *wicker-basket;* whence it has its name.

THE HAT-MAKER.

HATS are made either of wool, or hair of different animals, particularly of the beaver, rabbit, and camel. The process is nearly the same in all ; it will therefore be sufficient if we describe the method made use of in the manufacture of beaver hats.

The skin of the beaver is covered with two kinds of hair, the one long, stiff and glossy ; the other is short, thick and soft, and is alone used for hats.

To tear off one of these kinds of hair, and cut the other, women are employed, who make use of two knives : a large one something like a shoe-maker's knife, for the long hair ; and a smaller one nearly in the form of a pruning knife, with which they shave or scrape off the shorter hair.

When the hair is off, they mix and card it ; they then place it on a table having slits in it lengthwise : on this table they mix the hair together, the dust and filth falling through the chinks or slits. In this manner they form gores, as they are called, of an oval shape, and with the stuff that remains they supply and strengthen the parts that may be slighter than they should be. In that part of the brim which is next the crown, the substance is thicker than in the other parts of the hat.

The gores thus finished, the workman goes on to harden them into closer or more consistent flakes by pressure ; they are then carried to *the bason*, which is a sort of bench with an iron plate in it, and a little fire underneath it ; upon this the gores are laid, sprinkled, and brought into a conical shape by means of a mould.

The hat is now removed to a large receiver or trough, resembling a mill-hopper, to the bottom of which is attached a copper kettle filled with water and grounds, kept hot for the purpose. The *basoned hat* is first dipped in the kettle, and then worked for several hours, till it is properly thickened.

The hat is now to receive its due shape ; which is done by laying the conical cap on a wooden block of the size of the intended crown, tying it down fast with a piece of packthread at the bottom of the block ; after which it is singed, and the coarse knap is taken off, first with a pumice-stone, then with a piece of seal-skin ; and lastly, it is carded with a fine card to raise the cotton, with which the hat is afterwards to appear.

When the hat is so far advanced, it is sent, tied with the packthread on its block, to be dyed. This operation is performed by boiling 100 pounds of logwood, 12 pounds of gum, and 6 pounds of gall, in a proper quantity of water; after which 6 pounds of verdigrise, and 10 pounds of green vitriol, are added, and the liquor is kept simmering. Ten or twelve dozen of hats are immediately put in, each on its block, and kept down by cross bars for about an hour and a half: they are then taken out and aired, and the same number of other hats put in their room: the two sets of hats are then dipped and aired alternately several times each, the liquor being refreshed each time with more ingredients.

The dye being complete, the hatter hangs it in the roof of a stove or oven, at the bottom of which is a charcoal fire: when dry it is to be stiffened, which is done by melted glue or gum. It is then to be steamed on the *steaming-bason*, which is a little hearth or fire-place, raised three feet high, with an iron-plate laid over it, on which cloths, moistened with water, are laid, to secure the hat from burning. This operation is done entirely by the hand.

When steamed and dried, it is put again on the block, and brushed and ironed, on a table or bench, called the *stall-board*, till it receives the gloss which all new hats have. The edges are then clipped very smooth and even, and the lining sewed into the crown.

The figure in the back of the plate is the man at the trough, fulling and thickening the hat, which he does by rolling and unrolling it again and again in the hot liquor, first by his hands, and then by means of a little wooden roller.

The man at the stall-board is finishing a hat, after it has undergone the

operations of dyeing and steaming : he
is using the iron : the block belonging
to the hat under his hand stands at his
left hand, and the brush is before him.
Hats in an unfinished state are seen in
the left corner of the plate ; and on the
right are the boxes, ready to put the hats
into as soon as they are completed.

The hat-making business is reckoned
as good a one as almost any that is practised ; it is carred on with great success
in Bristol, and the surrounding villages.
An industrious journeyman will earn
two guineas a week.

THE JEWELLER.

It appears from history that the profession of a jeweller is of very ancient
date; for we read in the Bible that Aaron
had a breast-plate set with a variety of

W. sc.

Hat-maker.

Jeweller.

W.R. fc.

precious stones : and in succeeding ages there is frequent mention of rings and other ornaments being made of gold and set with stones. Hence the name jeweller, one who sets jewels, or precious stones, is properly derived. There is scarcely a nation in the world who have not employed jewellers of some kind or other. When captain Cook visited the South Sea islands, where, perhaps, no civilized being had been before, they found the natives with their ears, noses, and arms, ornamented with pearls, gold, shells, and curious teeth of fish, in a fanciful manner.

Civilized countries have greatly improved the art of jewellery. The French for lightness and elegance of design have surpassed their neighbours ; but the English jewellers, for excellence of workmanship, have been, and still are, superior to every other nation. The name jeweller is now commonly applied to all who set stones, whether real or artificial; but, properly speaking, it belongs only to those who set diamonds and other precious gems. According to the general application of the term, jewellers make rings of all sorts in gold, lockets, bracelets, broaches, ornaments for the head, ear-rings, necklaces, and a great variety of trinkets composed of *diamonds*, *pearls*, or other stones.

The DIAMOND was called by the antients *adamant :* as a precious stone, it holds the first rank, in value, hardness, and lustre, of all gems. The goodness of diamonds consists in their *water*, or colour, lustre and weight. The most perfect colour is the white. The defects in diamonds are veins, flaws, specks of red and black sand, and a blueish or yellowish cast.

In Europe, lapidaries examine the

goodness of their diamonds by daylight, but in the Indies they do it by night : for this purpose a hole is made in the wall, where a lamp is placed, with a thick wick, by the light of which they judge of the goodness of the stone.

Diamonds are found in the East Indies, principally in the kingdoms of Golconda, Visapour, Bengal, and the island of Borneo. They are obtained from mines and rivers.

As the diamond is the hardest of all precious stones, it can only be cut and ground by itself and its own substance. To bring diamonds to that degree of perfection which augments their price so considerably, the workmen rub several against each other; and the powder thus rubbed off the stones, and received in a little box for the purpose, serves to grind and polish others.

The PEARL is a hard, white, smooth,

shining body, found in shell-fish resembling an oyster, and is ranked among
the gems. The perfection of pearls,
whatever be their shape, consists chiefly
in the lustre and clearness of their colour,
which jewellers call their water. Those
which are white are the most esteemed in
Europe; while many Indians and the
Arabs prefer the yellow : some are of a
lead colour ; some border on the black,
and some are quite black. The *oriental*
pearls are the finest, on account of their
largeness, colour, and beauty, being generally of a beautiful silver white : those
found in the western hemisphere are
more of a milk-white.

In Europe *pearls* and *diamonds* are sold
by *carat* weight, the carat being equal
to four grains ; but in Asia, the weights
made use of are different in different
states.

In the print we have a man at work,

who will represent either a jeweller, or
a small worker in silver; one who makes
rings, perfume-boxes, &c. The board at
which he works is adapted also for a second workman. The leathern skins fastened to the board are to catch the filings
and small pieces of precious metals, which
would otherwise be liable to fall on the
ground. The tools on the board, and in
the front under the window, are chiefly
files of various kinds, and drills; beside
which there is a small hammer, a pair of
pliers, and, on a little block of wood, a
small crucible. On his left hand above
the board is a *drill bow:* this is a flexible
instrument, consisting of a piece of steel,
to the ends of which is fastened a cat-
gut: the cat-gut is twisted round one
of the drills which stand before the man,
and then it is fitted for his business.

Behind him is fixed the drawing-bench,
on which he draws out his wire to any

degree of fineness.   The method of
drawing wire from gold or other metals
is this : The metal is first made into a
cylindric form ; when it is drawn through
holes of several irons, each smaller than
the other, till it be as fine as it is wanted,
sometimes much smaller than a hair.
Every new hole lessens its diameter ;
but it gains in length what it loses in
thickness : a single ounce is frequently
drawn to a length of several thousand
feet.

In the front of the plate is represented a German stove, which is rarely
used for any other purpose than that of
heating the shop : for jewellers cannot
work in winter, unless the temperature
of the shop be pretty high.   At the top
of the stove is a crucible, and on the
floor is another : these are useful for
many purposes ; they are not however
heated in the stove, but in a *forge,* which

is an essential article in a jeweller's shop, though not exhibited in the plate.

Another very material tool found in every jeweller's work-room is the anvil and block.

A *flatting-mill* is also wanted, and indeed cannot be dispensed with where the business is considerable. The flatting-mill consists of two perfectly round and very highly polished rollers, formed internally of iron, and welded over with a plate of refined steel : the circumferences of these rollers nearly touch each other ; they are both turned with one handle. The lowermost roller is about ten inches in diameter, and the upper one is much smaller. The wire that is to be flattened, unwinding from a bobbin, and passing through a narrow slit in an upright piece of wood, called a *ketch,* is directed by a small conical hole in a piece of iron, called a *guide,* to any particular width of the rollers ; some of which, by means of this contrivance, are capable of receiving forty threads. After the wire is flatted, it is again wound on a bobbin, which is turned by a wheel, fixed on the axis of one of the rolls, and so managed that the motion of the bobbin just keeps pace with that of the rolls.

Besides those which are already mentioned, jewellers require a great variety of other tools ; such as *gravers, scorpers, spit-stickers, knife-tools, straining-weights, brass-stamps, lamp and blow-pipe, ring-sizes, spring-tongs, piercing-saws, boiling-pans, shears,* &c. &c.

The trade of a jeweller has always been considerable in London ; but, like many others, it is very much affected by a war, and at this moment it is exceedingly flat. During the American war, thousands of that business were almost in a starving condition : those only who are capable of turning their genius to other mechanical pursuits are likely to obtain employment at such times.

Some jewellers will earn as journey-men four guineas a week ; but the general run of wages is about 28 or 30 shillings.

———

THE BRICKLAYER.

THE bricklayer is an artificer who builds walls, &c. with bricks. In London this business includes tiling, walling, chimney-work, and paving with bricks and tiles. In the country, plaisterers' work is always joined to the business of a bricklayer, and not unfrequently stone-masons' work also.

The materials made use of by bricklayers are bricks, tiles, mortar, laths, nails, and tile-pins.

Their tools are a brick-trowel, to take up and spread the mortar; a brick-axe, to cut bricks to the proper shape and size; a saw is also occasionally wanted, and a stone to rub the bricks smooth when great exactness is required. A square is always wanted to lay the bed or foundation of any wall or building; a bevel, with which the under sides of the bricks are cut to a required angle; a piece of timber, called a *banker*—this is about six feet long, and laid on two other piers of timber, three feet high from the floor on which they stand, and on this they cut the bricks. Line-pins and a line are used to lay the courses or rows of bricks by; a plumb-rule, by which they carry their work upright. A level is wanted to conduct the building exactly horizontal; a small square to set off right angles; a ten-foot rod to take dimensions; and a jointer, or long flat

A Bricklayer.

WR. fc

lath about three inches wide, which is held by two men, while another draws the long joints ; a rammer, to render the foundation firm ; a crow, pick-axe, and shovel, with which they dig through and clear away any obstacles that may oppose their progress.

Bricks are made of clay in which are mixed ashes of sea-coal. By act of parliament bricks intended for sale must, when burned, be not less than $8\frac{1}{2}$ inches long, $2\frac{1}{2}$ inches thick, and 4 inches wide.

There are two kinds of bricks, called *stock-bricks* and *place-bricks*. The stock-bricks are the hardest, the most burnt, and used for the outside of walls ; and with the others the middle and inside work is wrought.

Bricklayers are supplied with bricks and mortar by a man they call a *labourer*, who is also employed in making the

mortar from lime. The labourer brings
the mortar, and the bricks, in a machine
called a hod, which he carries on his
shoulder. Before he puts the mortar
into the hod, he throws over every part
of the inner surface fine dry sand to prevent it from sticking to the wood.

A bricklayer and his labourer will lay
in a single day about a thousand bricks,
in what is called whole and solid work,
when the wall is either a brick and a
half or two bricks thick ; and since a
cubic yard contains 460 bricks, he will
lay above two cubic yards in a day.

The wages of a journeyman bricklayer are from four shillings to five
shillings and sixpence a day ; the wages
of a labourer, from half-a-crown to
three shillings and sixpence a day.

In the plate the bricklayer is building
a house : in his left hand is a brick, and
in his right the trowel : the trowel is

made of fine steel; and of so much importance is this instrument in the arts
of life, that the inventor of a new hammer, by which trowels are better and
more expeditiously made, has lately received forty guineas, as a reward for his
ingenuity, from the *Society of Arts, Manufactures, &c.* in the Adelphi. The
superior merit of trowels made by this
hammer consists in their great elasticity,
by which they always instantly return
to their original shape, although ever so
much bent out of it. The bricklayer is
standing on a scaffold: this consists of
upright poles to which two or more horizontal ones are tied at one end, having
the other fixed in the wall; and on these
flat boards are laid: at his right foot lies
his mortar, and on his left are his bricks;
but these cannot be seen in the plate.
On the ground the labourer is seen
making his mortar: near this the ladder

is placed, by which he and the bricklayer ascend the scaffold. His hod
rests against the end of the new building, and near the space left for the
lower window.

Bricklayers compute new work, such
as the walls of houses, &c. by the rod of
16½ feet, and the price charged includes
the putting up and use of scaffolding;
but the clearing out and carrying away
the rubbish is usually an extra charge.
In digging and steening of wells, the
work is charged at a certain price per
foot, and the price is higher for each
foot according as the depth is greater.

The emptying and carrying away soil,
that is to be removed for making foun-
dations or vaults, is charged by the ton:
eighteen cubic feet of soil is reckoned to
weigh a ton.

THE CARPENTER.

THERE is no art more useful than that which is exercised by the carpenter. It is his business to cut, fashion, and join timber and other wood for the purposes of building. There are several kinds of carpenters: but the term is usually applied to those who perform the rough work in the building of houses; such as hewing out, and putting in their places, the beams, rafters, joists, &c.: and those who do the lighter kind of work, as the making of doors, wainscoting and sashes, are called joiners: most of those, however, who are brought up to the trade are both carpenters and joiners.

The wood which they principally make use of is deal, oak, elm, and mahogany.

Deal is the wood of the fir tree, and

is chiefly brought from Sweden, Norway, and other northern European countries. The most common species of fir-trees are the *silver-leafed*, and the *pitch*, or Norway, or spruce fir. The first of these grow in many parts of Germany, from whence turpentine is sent into England ; but the most beautiful are those that grow on mount Olympus. The Norway fir produces the white deal commonly used by carpenters : from this pitch is also drawn ; whence it takes its second name.

Oak is too well known in this country to need any description ; it is chiefly used by ship-builders, of whom we shall speak hereafter.

Mahogany is a species of cedar : it is a native of the warmer parts of America, growing plentifully in the islands of Cuba, Jamaica, and Domingo. In some instances these trees grow to

A Carpenter.

WR *sc*

so large a size, as to be capable of being cut into planks of six feet in breadth : they rise to immense heights, notwithstanding they are sometimes found growing on rocks where there is scarcely any depth of earth.

The carpenter stands in need of a great variety of tools, such as saws, planes, chisels, hammers, awls, gimlets, &c. Common workmen are obliged to find their own tools, a set of which is worth from ten to twenty pounds, or even more. But for different kinds of mouldings, for beads, and fancy work, the master carpenter supplies his men with the necessary implements.

The practices in the art of carpentry and joinery are called planing, sawing, mortising, scribing, moulding, &c. The great difference in the trades of a carpenter, and a joiner, is, that the former is employed in the larger, stronger, and coarser operations, and the latter in the smaller and more curious works.

The carpenter in the plate is represented in the act of planing the edge of a board, that is held to the side of the bench by means of a screw which is always attached to it. On his bench are the hammer, pincers, mallet, and two chisels; a box also containing the turkey-stone with which he sharpens his tools : the shavings taken off by his plane are scattered on his bench and on the ground : at the right hand corner stand some boards, and his bag in which he carries his tools : on the other side is the saw, upon the four-legged stool which he uses for various purposes. Behind him is a new door, some other boards, a saw hanging against the wall, and a basket in which he puts his smaller tools.

He is represented preparing boards to

lay upon the roof of a new house in the back ground. The rafters are already in their places: the boards are to be laid next, in order to receive the slates.

The art of *sawing*, and the different kinds of saws made use of, will be described when we come to speak of the sawyer.

A *mortise* is a kind of joint, in which a hole of a certain depth is made in the thickness of a piece of wood, in order to receive another piece called a tenon.

Scribing is a term made use of when one side of a piece of stuff is to be fitted to the side of some other piece which is not regular. To make the two join close together all the way, the capenter *scribes* it; that is, he lays the piece of stuff to be *scribed* close to the other piece he intends to *scribe* to, and opens his compasses to the greatest distance the two pieces any where stand from each other; then bearing one of the legs against the side to be scribed to, with the other leg he draws a line on the stuff to be scribed. Thus he gets a line on the irregular piece parallel to the edge of the regular one; and if by a saw, or other instrument, the wood be cut exactly to the line, when the two pieces are put together they will make a neat joint.

Planing consists of taking off, as occasion may require, all the rough edges from wood, boards, &c. A plane consists of a piece of box-wood, very smooth at the bottom, serving as a stock, or shaft; in the middle of which is an aperture for a steel edge, or very sharp chisel, to pass. This edge is easily adjusted by a stroke of the hammer at one of the ends of the stock.

Planes have different names, according to their forms, sizes, and uses; as the

Jack-plane, which is about eighteen inches long, and intended for the roughest kind of work:

The *long-plane* is two feet in length: it smooths the work after the rough stuff is taken off: it is one of this kind that the carpenter in the plate is represented as using, and it is well adapted for smoothing the edges of boards that are to be joined:

The *smoothing-plane* is only six or seven inches long, and is used on almost all occasions:

The *rabbet-plane* cuts the upper edge of a board straight or square, down into the stuff, so that the edge of another, cut after the same manner, may join with it on the square.

Besides these there are *ploughing-planes, moulding-planes, round-planes, hollow-planes, snipe's-bill-planes,* &c.

Glue is a very important article in the carpenter's and joiner's trade. It is made

of the skins of all kinds of beasts, reduced to the state of jelly ; and the older
the animal, the better is the glue that
is made of its hide.

A ship-carpenter is an officer at sea,
whose business consists in having things
in readiness for keeping the vessel in
which he is stationed, in repair ; and in
attending to the stopping of leaks, to
caulking*, careening, and the like.   He
is to watch the timber of the vessel, to
see that it does not rot; and in time
of battle he is to have every thing prepared for repairing and stopping breach-
es made by the enemy's cannon.

A journeyman carpenter, when he
works by the day, receives from three
shillings and sixpence to four shillings
and sixpence a day.

---

* These terms will be explained in the article de-
voted to the ship-wright.

THE COOPER.

A COOPER manufactures casks, tubs of all sizes, pails, and sundry other articles useful in domestic concerns. These are made with oak timber, a great part of which comes from America, cut up into narrow pieces called staves; they are sometimes bent, and for other sorts of work they are straight. For tubs, pails, &c. the bottoms of which are less than the tops, the staves are wider at top than they are at the bottom. These staves are kept together by means of hoops, which are made of hazel and ash; but some articles require iron hoops. To make them hold water or other liquids, the cooper places between each stave from top to bottom split flags, which swell with moisture, and effectually prevent the vessel from leaking.

The tools required by the cooper are numerous, some of which are peculiar to his art; but most of them are common both to him and the carpenter.

In the plate we see the cooper busily employed in putting together a hogshead. In his left hand he holds a flat piece of wood, which he lays on the edge of the hoop, while he strikes it with the hammer in his right hand. To make the hoops stick, he takes the precaution to chalk the staves before he begins this part of the operation. The tops and bottoms he puts together by means of wooden pegs.

Around the wall of the shop, and on the floor, we see the iron and wooden hoops, and various tools, such as saws, axes, spoke-shaves, stocks and bits adzes, augers, &c. &c. The structure and uses of the saw and the axe are too well known to stand in need of description.

A Cooper

W.fc.

Spoke-shaves are of different kinds; they are intended for uses similar to those for which the carpenter adapts his planes: two of them are represented in the plate: one hangs by a handle not far from the right hand of the cooper; and the other lies on the large block of wood, which is useful for various purposes.

The *stock-and-bit* make but one instrument; it hangs over the left shoulder of the cooper. The stock is the handle, and the bit is a sort of piercer that fits into the bottom of the stock: bits of various sorts are adapted to the same stock: of course, the bit is always moveable, and may instantly be replaced by one of a different bore.

An *adze* is a cutting tool of the axe kind, having its blade made very thin and arching: it is used chiefly for taking off thin chips, and for cutting the hollow sides of boards, &c.

Augers, or, as they are sometimes spelt, *awgres*, are used for boring large holes : they are a kind of large gimlet, consisting of a wooden handle, and an iron blade which is terminated with a steel bit. One of these instruments hangs between the saw and stock-and-bit, but above them ; and two others of different kinds are near the right hand of the cooper.

The trade of the cooper was formerly among the cries of London ; " Any work for the cooper ?" is now heard in many parts of the country. A travelling cooper carries with him a few hoops of different sizes, some iron rivets, and wooden pegs, his hammer, adze, and stock-and-bit. With these few instruments he can repair all washing and brewing utensils, besides the churns and wooden vessels made use of dairies. An ingenious working cooper will in his peregrinations readily perform sundry jobs that belong to the carpenter, in villages which are too small to support a person in that trade. A journeyman cooper, who works for a master, will earn from three to five shillings per day.

Every custom-house and excise-office has an officer called the *king's-cooper ;* and every large ship has a cooper on board, whose business is to look after all the casks intended for water, beer, and spirits.

THE STONE-MASON.

THE business of the stone-mason consists in the art of hewing or squaring stones and marble ; in cutting them for the purposes of building, and in being able to work them up with mortar.

When the stones are large, the busi-

ness of hewing and cutting them belongs
to the *stone-cutter;* but these are frequently ranked with the masons, and so
also are those who fashion the ornaments
of sculpture though they are properly
carvers and sculptors in stone.

The tools principally used by masons
are the square, level, plumb-line, bevel,
compass, hammer, chisel, mallet, saw,
and trowel.

The mason in the front of the plate
is carving a stone with a *mallet* and *chisel:* before him, and on the block of
stone which supports the piece on which
he is at work, lies his *bevel:* the two
sides of the bevel move on a joint, so
that they may be set to any angle. When
masons or bricklayers speak of a *bevel*
angle, they mean one which is neither
forty-five nor ninety degrees.

In the back-ground of the picture
there is a man sawing into thin pieces

a large block of stone. The stone-mason's saw is different from those used by other mechanics ; it has no teeth ; and, being moved backwards and forwards by a single man, it cuts the stone by its own weight. In winter time, and in rainy or very sultry weather, the sawyer sits in a wooden box, not unlike a watchman's box, but without a front to it. These boxes are moveable, so that the workman may secure himself from the piercing blasts of winter, and the scorching sun-beams in summer.

Both marble and stone are dug out of quarries : the grain of marble is so fine as readily to take a beautiful polish. It is of course much used in ornaments of buildings, as columns, statues, altars, tombs, chimney-pieces, tables, &c.

There are an indefinite number of different kinds of marbles, and they take their name either from their colour, their age, their country, their degree of hardness, or their defects. Some are of one colour only, as black or white ; others are streaked or variegated with stains, clouds, and veins ; but almost all are opake, excepting the white, which when cut into very thin slices and polished becomes transparent.

Marble is polished by being first rubbed with free-stone, afterwards with pumice-stone, and lastly with emery or calcined tin. Artificial marble is real marble pulverized and mixed with plaster ; and from this composition are made statues, busts, basso-relievos, and other ornaments of architecture.

Few natural substances are less understood than marble : the people who are accustomed to work them, know from experience, and at first sight, that one sort will receive a high polish ; that another is easily wrought ; and a third refuses the tools. And men of science know little more.

Masons make use of several kinds of stone, but *Portland-stone* is the principal : of this there are vast quarries in the island of Portland in Dorsetshire, from whence it is brought in large quantities to London. It is used for building in general ; for copings at the tops of houses, and as supports for iron rails ; for window cills ; for stone balusters ; for steps and paving where great neatness is required.

This stone is very soft when it comes out of the quarry ; it works easily, and becomes hard by length of time. The piers and arches of Westminster bridge are built with it ; and so is the magnificent cathedral of St. Paul's.

Purbeck-stone comes from an island of that name also in Dorsetshire ; it is chiefly used in paving, steps, and other rough work.

Yorkshire-stone is also used for paving, steps, coping, and other purposes in which strength and durability are required. There is also a stone which, when cut into slabs, is used for hearths, called *Ryegate-stone*.

Stone-masons make use of *mortar, plaster of Paris,* and *tarrass,* for cementing or joining their works. The two former are used in dry work, and the latter for bridges and buildings exposed to the water.

Mortar is a composition of lime and sand mixed to a proper consistency with water.

Plaster of Paris is made by burning a stone called gypsum.

Tarrass is a coarse sort of plaster, or mortar, durable in wet: it is chiefly used to line basons, cisterns, wells, and other reservoirs of water. That which is called Dutch tarrass is made of a soft rock-stone, found near Cologne on the Rhine : it is burnt like lime, and reduced to powder by mills, and from thence carried to Holland, where it has acquired the name of Dutch tarrass. It is very dear, on account of the great demand there is for it in aquatic works.

An artificial tarrass is formed of two parts of lime and one of plaster of Paris; and another consists of one part of lime and two parts of well sifted coal-ashes. These are all used occasionally by the mason and bricklayer.

Stone-masons measure and charge their work either by the superficial or cubic foot : they have extra charges for iron cramps, which fasten two or more stones together; for cutting holes in which iron rails are fixed, and for various other things.

The journeyman mason has about 4s. or 4s. 6d. per day, and the labourer

from 2s. 6d. to 3s. per day : but others
who work by the piece, or who are employed in carving or other fine work,
will earn more than double that sum.

THE SAWYER.

In the early periods of the world,
the trunks of trees were split with
wedges into as thin pieces as possible
by that mode ; and if it were necessary
to have them still thinner, they were
hewn on both sides by hatchets, till they
were reduced to a proper size.   The
common saw, which requires only to be
guided by the hand of the workman,
was not known in America when it was
discovered and subjugated by Euro-
peans.

The saw is, undoubtedly, one of the
most useful instruments in the mechanic

Stone-mason.

WR *sc.*

A Sawyer.

arts, ever invented. Among the Greeks, the inventor has been enrolled in their mythology with a place among the gods, and honoured as one of the greatest benefactors of the human race. The invention is attributed to Icarus the son of Dædalus, who is said to have taken the first hint from the spine or backbone of a flat-fish.

The best *saws* are of tempered steel, ground bright and polished: the edge, in which the teeth are, is always thicker than the back. The teeth are cut and sharpened by a triangular file. When filed, the teeth are to be *set*, that is, turned askew, or out of a right line, to make the fissure wider, that the back may follow with ease. This is done by putting an instrument between every two teeth, and giving it a little wrench, which turns one of the teeth in one direction, and the other in a contrary one.

The teeth are always set *ranker* for coarse cheap work, than for that which is hard and fine.

The *pit-saw*, such as is represented in the plate, is a large two-handed saw used to saw timber in pits. It is set rank for coarse stuff, so as to make a fissure of almost a quarter of an inch.

The sawyer cuts the trunks of trees into beams and planks, fit for the use of carpenters. The timber is laid on a frame over an oblong pit, called a saw-pit; and it is cut by means of a long saw fastened in a frame, which is worked up and down by two men, one standing on the wood to be cut, and the other in the pit. As they proceed in their work, they drive wedges at a proper distance from the saw to keep the fissure open; which enables the saw to move with freedom.

This is a very laborious employment,

and two industrious men may earn from
twelve to eighteen shillings a day.

That the saws of the Grecian carpenters were of a similar form to the common pit-saw now in use, is manifest
from a painting preserved among the
antiquities of Herculaneum. In this,
the piece of wood to be sawn is secured
by cramps. The saw consists of a square
frame, having in the middle a blade, and
it very much resembles the figure of the
saw in the plate. The piece of wood
extends beyond the end of the bench,
and one of the workmen appears standing, and the other sitting on the ground.
The pit used in modern times is a great
improvement, as the power of a man
standing in the pit, must far exceed that
exerted by him in a sitting posture.

The most beneficial and ingenious
improvement of this instrument was the
invention of *saw-mills*, which are worked

either by water, by wind, or by steam.

A saw-mill consists of several parallel saws, which are made to rise and fall perpendicularly by means of a mechanical motion. A very few hands are necessary to conduct this operation, to push forward the pieces of timber, which are either laid on rollers, or suspended by ropes, in proportion as the sawing advances.

But the sawing machines worked by steam in the *block-house* in Portsmouth dock-yard, convey to the spectator the nature of mechanical operations in the completest manner possible. The manufacture of blocks in that place cannot fail to interest every one who has the slightest turn for mechanics, and a person must be devoid of all curiosity, who can visit Portsmouth and return without making every effort to be introduced into this part of the dock-yard.

THE SMITH.

A SMITH is one who works on iron, and who from that metal manufacture a vast variety of articles useful in the arts of life, and of great importance to domestic comfort. There are several branches in this trade : some are called *black-smiths*, and of this class is the man represented in the plate : others are called *white-smiths*, or *bright-smiths ;* these polish their work to a considerable degree of nicety : some include in their business bell-hanging, which is now carried to great perfection : others are chiefly employed in the manufacture of locks and keys.

In the smith's shop there must be a forge, an anvil and block, a vice fastended to an immoveable bench, besides hammers, tongs, files, punches, and pincers, of different sorts.

The *forge* is the most prominent article; it is represented in the plate on
the left hand of the smith. The forge
is a sort of furnace intended for heating
metals so hot as to render them mal-
leable, and fit to be formed into various
shapes. The back of the forge is built
upright to the ceilion, and is enclosed
over the fire-place with a *hovel*, which
leads into the chimney to carry away the
smoke. In the back of the forge, against
the fire-place, is a thick iron plate with
a pipe fixed to it to receive the nose of
the bellows. The bellows are behind
the forge: these are worked by means
of a *rocker*, with a string or chain fastened to it, which the smith or his labourer pulls. One of the boards of the
bellows is fixed, and by drawing down
the handle of the rocker the moveable
board rises, and by means of a weight
on the top of the upper-board sinks

A Smith.

WP sc.

again; and by this alternate motion the fire is raised to any degree of heat.

In the front of the forge, and a little below it, is a *trough of water*, which is useful for wetting the coals to make them throw out a greater heat; the water serves also for cooling the tongs, with which the smith holds the heated iron, and which in a short time become too hot for him to grasp: the smith likewise hardens his iron by dipping it while red-hot in the water-trough.

The smith in the plate is represented in the act of forging a piece of iron, which he has just taken from the fire with the tongs in his left hand. Iron is hammered or forged two ways: either by the force of the hand, in which there are sometimes several persons employed, one holding and turning the iron, and hammering likewise, while the others hammer only, with what are called sledge hammers, such as that which stands on the ground of the plate resting against the block : or, it is done by the force of a water-mill, which raises and works several enormous hammers : under the strokes of these the men have only to present the large lumps of iron, which are sustained at one end by the anvils, and at the other by iron chains fastened to the ceiling of the forge. This last method is employed in the largest works, such as the making of anchors of ships, which weigh several thousand pounds.

In lighter works, such as we have in the plate—namely, in the making of stoves, shovels, gridirons, trivets, &c. &c. —a single man is sufficient to hold, to heat, and to turn the iron with one hand, while he strikes it with the other.

The several heats given by smiths to their iron are called the *blood-red* heat, the *white* heat, and the *welding* heat.

The blood-red heat is used when the iron has already acquired its form and size, but wants hammering only to smooth and fit it for the file.

The white heat is used when the iron has not its form and size, but must be forged into both.

The welding heat is required when two pieces of iron are to be united end to end.

The uppermost surface of the *anvil*, on which a smith hammers his iron, must be very flat and smooth, and so hard that no file will touch it. At one end of the anvil is a hole, in which may be placed a strong steel chisel, or spike; on this a piece of red-hot iron may be laid, and cut in two with a single stroke of the hammer. Anvils are sometimes made of cast iron; but the best are those which are forged, with the upper part made of steel. The whole is usually mounted on a firm wooden block.

The *vice* fixed to the bench serves to hold any thing upon which the smith is at work, whether it requires filing, or bending, or riveting. There are hand vices, and small anvils, which are occasionally used in the more delicate operations of this business.

Square and flat bars of iron are sometimes twisted for ornamental work : this is done by giving the metal a white heat, fixing it in the vice, and turning it with the tongs.

Iron rails before houses are generally made of cast iron, which is run from the ore, and neither requires nor will bear the hammer : it is brittle, and will not yield in the least to the file. It is the business of the black-smith to make the upper rail to receive these bars, and to fix them into the stone-work.

It would be impossible to enumerate all the articles manufactured by the smith: they are of all kinds, and of almost all values. I have seen a steel stove made at Brodie's manufactory in Carey-street, of several hundred pounds value: and a more interesting sight cannot well be viewed than the store-rooms of our large furnishing ironmongers.

Iron is dug out of the bowels of the earth in many parts of this kingdom; but great quantities are imported, from Sweden and North America, in pigs and bars.

Black-smiths charge for hammered work, such as rails, window-bars, &c. six-pence per lb.; for ornamental work, as brackets, lamp-irons, &c. from eight-pence to fourteen-pence per lb.; and cast iron rails, sash-weights, &c. about fifteen or eighteen shillings per hundred weight.

A journeyman smith will earn from three to five shillings per day; but those who work on the fine polished articles will earn much higher wages.

———

THE SHIP-WRIGHT.

A SHIP has been defined, a timber building, consisting of various parts and pieces, nailed and pinned together with iron and wood, in such form as to be fit to float, and to be conducted by wind and sails from sea to sea.

The word *ship* is a general name for all large vessels with sails, adapted for navigation on the sea : but by sailors the term is more particularly applied to a vessel furnished with three masts, each

Shipwright

WR. sc.

of which is composed of a lower-mast, a
top-mast, and a top-gallant-mast.

A *ship-wright* is one who is employed
in building or repairing such vessels.
Ship-building is to this country one of
the most important arts; it is studied as
a science by the learned, who denomi-
nate it *naval architecture:* for the pro-
motion of this science, a very respectable body of ingenious men have for the
last fifteen years associated.

In ship-building three things are necessary to be considered: First, to give
the vessel such a form as shall be best
adapted for sailing, and for the service
for which she is designed: secondly, to
unite the several parts into a compact
frame; and thirdly, to provide suitable
accommodations for the officers and
crew, as well as for the cargo, furniture,
provisions, guns, and ammunition.

The outside figure of a ship includes

the bottom, or the hold, which is the part that is under the water when the vessel is laden ; and the upper works are called the *dead works*, which are usually above the water when the ship is laden.

To give a proper shape to the bottom of the ship, it is necessary to consider the service for which she is designed. A *ship of war* should be able to sail swiftly, and carry her lower tier of guns four or five feet out of the water : a *merchant-ship* ought to be able to contain a large cargo of goods, and to be navigated with few hands ; and both should be able to carry sail firmly ; to steer well ; and to sustain the shocks of the sea without being violently strained.

Ships are built principally with *oak* timber, which is the stoutest and strongest wood we have, and therefore best fitted both to keep sound under water, and to bear the blows and shocks of the waves,

and the terrible strokes of cannon-balls.
For this last purpose, it is a peculiar excellence of the oak, that it is not so liable
to splinter or shiver as other wood, so
that a ball can pass through it without
making a large hole. The great use of
the oak for the structure of merchant-
ships, as well as for men of war, is re-
ferred to by Mr. Pope :

> While by our oaks the precious loads are borne,
> And realms commanded which those trees adorn.

During the construction of a ship, she
is supported in the dock, or upon a wharf,
by a number of solid blocks of timber
placed at equal distances from and parallel to each other ; in which situation she
is said to be on the stocks.

The first piece of timber laid upon the
blocks is generally the *keel,* which, at one
end, is let into the stern-post, and at the
other into the *stem.* If the carcase of a
ship be compared to the skeleton of a

human body, the *keel* may be considered as the back-bone, and the timbers as the ribs.

The *stern* is the hinder part of the ship, near which are the state-room, cabins, &c. To the stern-post is fixed the iron-work that holds the *rudder*, which directs the course of the vessel.

The *stem* is a circular piece of timber in the front; into this the sides of the ship are inserted. The outside of the stem is usually marked with a scale or division of feet, according to its perpendicular height from the keel; the intention of this is to ascertain the draught of water at the fore-part, when the ship is in preparation for a sea voyage.

In the plate the ship-wright is represented standing at the stern on a scaffold, and driving in the wedges with his wooden trunnel. The holes are first bored with the auger, and then the wedges

drove in; these are afterwards cut off with
a saw. At his feet lie his saw; his auger,
which is used for boring large holes; his
axe, and punches of different sizes.

The *caulking* of a ship is a very important operation : it consists in driving
oakum, or the substance of old ropes un-
twisted, and pulled into loose hemp, into
the seams of the planks, to prevent the
ship's leaking. It is afterwards covered
with hot melted pitch, or rosin, to prevent
its rotting.

A mixture, used for covering the bottom of ships, is made of one part of tallow,
one of brimstone, and three parts of
rosin : this is called *paying* the bottom.
The sides are usually *payed* with tar,
turpentine, or rosin.

To enable ships to sail well, the out-
sides in contact with the water are frequently covered with copper.

The masts of ships are made of *fir* or

pine, on account of the straightness and lightness of that wood: the length of the *main-mast* of an East India ship is about eighty feet. The masts always bear a certain proportion to the breadth of the ship : whatever the breadth of the ship be, multiply that breadth by twelve, and divide the product by five, which gives the *length* of the *main-mast*. Thus, a ship which measures thirty feet at the broadest part will have a main-mast seventy-two feet long: the thickness of the mast is estimated by allowing one inch for every three feet in length : accordingly, a mast seventy-two feet long must be twenty-four inches thick. For the other masts different proportions are to be used. To the masts are attached the yards, sails, and rigging, which receive the wind necessary for navigation.

In a dock-yard where ships are built, six or eight men, called *quartermen*, are frequently intrusted to build a ship, and engage to perform the business for a certain sum, under the inspection of a master buildier.   These employ other men under them, who, according to their different departments, will earn from fifteen or twenty shillings to two or three pounds per week.

When a ship is finished building it is to be *launched*, that is, put out of dock. To render the operation of launching easy, the ship when first built is supported by two strong platforms laid with a gradual inclination to the water. Upon the surface of this declivity are placed two corresponding ranges of planks, which compose the base of the frame, called the *cradle*, to which the ship's bottom is securely attached.   The planes of the cradle and platform are well greased, and then the *blocks* and *wedges*, by which the ship was supported, are driven

out from under the keel; afterwards the
shores, by which she is retained on the
stocks, are cut away, and the ship slides
down to the water.

Ships of the first rate are usually con-
structed in dry docks, and afterwards
floated out, by throwing open the flood-
gates, and sufferlng the tide to enter, as
soon as they are finished.

THE MARINER.

A MARINER is in common language
the same as sailor or seaman. Mariners
are sometimes employed on board merchant ships, and sometimes in men of war.
In merchants' employ, the mariners are
accountable to the master, the master to
the owners of the vessel, and the owners
to the merchant, for any damages that
may happen. If a vessel is lost by tem-

Mariner.

WR. sc.

pest, the mariners lose their wages, and the owners their freight: this is intended to make them use their utmost endeavours to preserve the ship committed to their care.

Mariners on board the king's ships are subject to strict regulations, which, however, depend on certain fixed laws passed at different times by parliament. Mariners who are not in His Majesty's service are liable during the time of war to be impressed, unless they enter voluntarily, to which they are encouraged by bounties and high wages: and every foreign seaman, who, during war shall serve two years in any man of war, merchantman, or privateer, becomes naturalized.

The mariner represented in the plate is of a higher rank and estimation than common sailors: he understands the art of navigation, or of conducting a vessel from one place to another, in the safest, shortest, and most commodious way. He ought therefore to be well acquainted with the islands, rocks, sands, and straits, near which he has to sail. He should also know the signs which indicate the approach to land : these are, the appearing of birds ; the floating of weeds on the surface of the sea ; the depth and colour of the sea. He should, moreover, understand the nature of the winds, particularly the times when the *trade* winds and monsoons set in ; the seasons when storms and hurricanes may be expected, and the signs of their approach ; the motion of currents and of tides. He must understand also the working of a ship ; that is, the management of the sails, rigging, &c.

Navigation, or the proper employment of the mariner, is either *common* or *proper*. The former is usually called coasting ; that is, where the ships are on the same, or very neighbouring coasts; and where the vessel is seldom out of sight of land, or out of reach of *sounding*. In this case, little more is required than an acquaintance with the lands they have to pass, the compass, and the sounding-line.

To gain a knowledge of the coast, a good chart or map is necessary.

The *compass*, or mariner's compass, as it is usually called, is intended to direct and ascertain a ship's course at sea. It consists of a circular brass box, which contains a card, with the thirty.two points of the compass fixed on a magnetic needle that always turns to the north, or nearly so. The needle with the card turns on an upright pin fixed in the centre of the box.

The top of the box is covered with glass, to prevent the wind from disturbing the motion of the card. The whole is inclosed in another box of wood, where it is suspended by brass hoops to keep the card in a horizontal position, whatever the motion of the ship may be: and it is so placed in the ship, that the middle section of the box may lie over the middle section of the ship along its keel.

The method of finding, by the compass, the direction in which a ship sails, is this: The compass being suspended, the mariner looks horizontally over it in the direction of the ship's *wake**, by which he sees the point of the compass denoting the direction of the wake; the point opposite to this is that to which the ship is sailing according to the compass; and knowing how much the compass varies, he can tell the true point of the horizon to which he is going.

The *sounding-line* is a line with a plummet at the end: it is used to try

---

* The *wake* of a ship is the print or track impressed by the course of a ship on the surface of the water.

the depth of the water and the quality
of the bottom.

In *Navigation proper*, which is where
the voyage is long, and pursued through
the main ocean, there are many other
requisites wanted besides those already
mentioned. Here a considerable skill in
practical mathematics and astronomy is
required, and an aptness in using instruments for celestial observations.

One of these instruments the mariner
in the plate is represented holding in his
right hand, while he is pointing to his
ship with the other. The boat which is
to carry him on board the ship is drawn
to shore.

At a distance in the sea is represented
a *light-house*, erected on a rock, and
having in the night a fire or other considerable light at the top, so as to be seen
at a great distance from land. The use
of the light-house is to direct the ships

on the coast, to prevent them from running on the shore, and from other injuries by an improper course.

The wages of a mariner depend upon his employment, that is, whether he be in the King's service or on board a merchantman : they depend also upon the size of the ship, and upon the situation which he holds in it.

There is no profession of more importance to the interests of this country than that of the mariner. Government therefore provides, for those who are disabled, a place in Greenwich Hospital ; and to the widows and children of those who are slain in defending their country, small pensions are granted. Greenwich Hospital is supported by the nation, and by sixpence a month deducted out of every seaman's wages.

THE CURRIER.

THE business of the CURRIER is to prepare hides, which have been under the hands of the tanner, for the use of shoemakers, coachmakers, sadlers, bookbinders, &c.

Currying is the last preparation, and puts the leather into a condition to be made up into shoes, saddles, harness, &c., and is performed two ways, either upon the *flesh* or the *grain*.

In dressing leather for shoes *on the flesh*, the first operation is soaking the leather in water, until it be thoroughly wet; then the flesh side is shaved on a beam, that is, a sort of wooden block fixed on the ground to which the currier stands at his work, with a knife of a peculiar construction, and which indeed varies in different places. This is one

of the most curious and laborious operations in the art of currying.

The knife used for this purpose is of a
rectangular form, with two handles, one
at each end, and a double edge.   The
best knives are said to be manufactured
at Cirencester, and composed of iron and
steel : the edge is made by rubbing them
on a flat stone of a gritty substance till
it comes to a kind of wire ; the wire is
taken off by a finer stone, and the edge
is then turned to a kind of groove wire
by a piece of steel in form of a bodkin ;
this steel is used to renew the edge in
the operation.

After the leather is properly shaved,
it is thrown into water again, and
scoured upon a board or stone appropriated to the use.   Scouring is performed by rubbing the grain or hair
side with a piece of pumice-stone*, or

* Perhaps the idea, which led to the patent lately taken out for the new mode of *shaving*, was taken

some other stone of a good grit, by which means a white sort of substance is forced out of the leather, called the *bloom*, produced in the operation of tanning. The hide is then conveyed to the shade, or drying-place, when the oily substances are applied, which are put on both sides of the leather, but in a greater and thicker quantity on the flesh side than on the hair side.

When it is quite dry, it undergoes other operations for the purpose of softening the leather. Whitening or parting succeeds, which is performed with a fine edge on the knife already described. It is then *boarded up*, or grained again, by applying the graining-board, first to the grain side and then to the flesh side.

from this part of the currier's business : the patentee at least expected to shave the public.——See **Monthly Magazine, vol. xvii. p. 477.**

It is now fit for *waxing*, which is performed by rubbing it with a brush, dipped in a composition of oil and lampblack, on the flesh side, till it be thoroughly black : it is then *sized*, called black sizing, with a brush or sponge, dried and tallowed.   After undergoing some other operations, this sort of leather, called waxed leather, is *curried*.

For leather curried on the hair side, termed black on the grain, the first operation is the same with that already described, till it is scoured.   Then the black is applied to it while wet, which is a solution of copperas in water : this is first put upon the grain, after it has been rubbed over with a brush dipped in urine; and when it is dry it is *seasoned*, that is, rubbed over with a brush, dipped in copperas water on the grain, till it be perfectly black : after this, the grain is raised with a fine graining-board, and the leather is oiled with a mixture of oil and tallow, when it is finished, and fit for the shoe-maker.

Hides are sometimes *curried* for the use of sadlers and collar-makers, but the principal operations are much the same as those which have been already described. Hides for the roofs of coaches are shaved nearly as thin as those for shoes, and blacked on the grain.

In the plate we see the currier engaged in his business: on his right hand and on his left are hides which have undergone part of the operation; and behind him, pinned to the wall, are two skins finished except the drying.

In many places, the business of the currier connects with it that of the leather-dresser and leather-cutter, who supplies the shoe makers and others with all their leather, black, red, blue, green, &c.

Leadenhall Market is one of the principal marts for leather ; and shoe-makers, and leather-cutters in the country, who can command the capital, buy the greater part of their goods, particularly their sole-leather, there.

The curriers have been an incorporated company ever since the beginning of the reign of James the First : and during the reign of Queen Elizabeth, history records an account of a fierce contention between the curriers and shoemakers, respecting the dressing of leather and the price to be paid them for their work ; and also respecting the places in which leather should be sold. At length it was stipulated, in the year 1590, among other articles, that the curriers should have the dressing of all the leather brought into Leadenhall and Southwark Markets, and within three miles of London.

The use of skins is very antient, the

Currier.

WR. Sc.

Apothecary.

WR. sc.

first garments in the world having been made of them. *Moroccoes* are made of the skins of a kind of goats. Parchment is made of sheep-skins. The true shammy leather is made of the skin of an animal of the same name, though it is frequently counterfeited with common goat's and sheep skin.

The Indian women in Carolina and Virginia dress buck-and doe-skins with a considerable degree of skill; and so quick that a single woman will completely dress eight or ten skins in a day.

THE APOTHECARY.

THE office of the APOTHECARY is to attend on sick persons, and to prepare and give them medicines, either on his own judgment or according to the prescription of the physician.

It is well known that the word *apo-
theca* signified originally any kind of
store, magazine, or warehouse; and
that the proprietor or keeper of such a
store was called *apothecarius.* We must
not, therefore, understand by the word,
when mentioned in writings two or three
hundred years old, apothecaries such as
ours are at present. At those periods,
persons were often called apothecaries,
who at courts, and in the houses of great
people, prepared for the table various
preserves, particularly fruit incrusted
with sugar, and who on that account
may be considered as confectioners.
Hence, perhaps, we see the reason why
apothecaries were in this country combined with the *grocers,* till the reign of
James the First. They were then sepa-
rated, and the apothecaries were incorporated as a company: the reason as-
signed for this was, that medicines

might be better prepared, and that un-
wholesome remedies might not be im-
posed on the sick.

From this period, apothecaries were
distinguished for selling drugs used in
medicine, and preparing from them different compounds, according to the pre-
scriptions given by physicians and others.
Prior to this, it is probable, physicians
usually prepared their own medicines;
and it has been thought that they gradu-
ally became accustomed to employ apothecaries for the sake of their own convenience, when they found in their
neighbourhood a druggist in whose skill
they could confide, and whose interest
they wished to promote, by resigning in
his favour that part of the occupation.

Such an employment as that of an
apothecary is, however, mentioned at a
much earlier period of our history; for
it is said, that King Edward the Third

gave a pension of sixpence a day to
Coursus de Gangeland, an apothecary
in London, for taking care of and attending his majesty during his illness in
Scotland; and this is the first mention
of an apothecary.

In the year 1712 the importance of
this profession was acknowledged by an
act of parliament, which exempted for
a limited time apothecaries from serving
the offices of constable, and scavenger,
and other ward and parish offices, and
from serving upon juries; which act was
a few years afterwards made perpetual.

The apothecaries, as a body, have a
hall near Bridge-street, Black-friars,
where there are two magnificent labora-
tories, out of which all the surgeons'
chests are supplied with medicines for
the British navy. Here also drugs of all
sorts are sold to the public, which may
be depended upon as pure and unadul-

terated. But as almost all persons who practise in this profession are men of liberal education, and acquainted with the theory and practice of chemistry, there are very few of them who do not prepare their own drugs, either wholly or in part.

In many places, and particularly in opulent cities, the first apothecaries' shops were established at the public expense, and belonged, in fact, to the magistrates. A particular garden also was often appropriated to the use of the apothecary, in order that he might rear in it the necessary plants, and which was therefore called the apothecaries' garden.

In conformity to this principle, Sir Hans Sloane, in the year 1721, presented the apothecaries' company with a spacious piece of ground at Chelsea, for a physic garden, on condition of their paying the small ground rent of 5*l.* per annum; of continuing it always as a physic garden, and of presenting to the Royal Society fifty samples of different sorts of plants grown there, till they amounted to two thousand. The latter of these conditions has been long since more than completed.

In this garden there are two very magnificent cedars, which were planted in 1683, and were then about three feet high. The pine-tree, coffee-tree, tea-shrub, and sugar-cane, are among the curiosities which may be seen at this place.

This is a very genteel business; and a youth intended to be an apothecary should be a good scholar, at least he should know as much of Latin as to be able to read the best writers in the various sciences connected with medicine.

All persons apprenticed to an apothecary are bound for eight years. An as-

sistant, or journeyman, to an apothecary
will have from forty to fourscore pounds
per annum, exclusive of his board.

THE BAKER.

THE chief art of the BAKER consists
in making bread, rolls, and biscuits, and
in baking various kinds of provisions.

It is not known when this very useful
business first became a particular profession. Bakers were a distinct body of
people in Rome nearly two hundred
years before the Christian æra, and it is
supposed that they came from Greece.
To these were added a number of free-
men, who were incorporated into a *college*, from which neither they nor their
children were allowed to withdraw.
They held their effects in common,
without enjoying any power of parting

with them. Each bake house had a *pa-tron*, who had the superintendency of it; and one of the patrons had the management of the others, and the care of the college. So respectable were the bakers at Rome, that occasionally one of the body was admitted among the senators.

Even by our own statutes the bakers are declared not to be handicrafts; and in London they are under the particular jurisdiction of the lord mayor and aldermen, who fix the price of bread, and have the power of finding these who do not conform to their rules.

Bread is made of flour mixed and kneaded with yeast, water, and a little salt. It is known in London under two names, the *white* or *wheaten*, and the *household:* these differ only in degrees of purity; and the loaves must be mark-

Baker.

WR. sc.

ed with a W or H, or the Baker is liable
to suffer a penalty.

The process of bread-making is thus
described :—To a peck of meal are added a handful of salt, a pint of yeast, and
three quarts of water, cold in summer,
hot in winter, and temperate between
the two. The whole being kneaded, as
is represented in the plate, will rise in
about an hour; it is then moulded into
loaves, and put into the oven to bake.

The oven takes more than an hour to
heat properly, and bread about three
hours to bake. Most bakers make and
sell rools in the morning : these are either *common*, or *French* rools: the former
differ but little from loaf-bread : the ingredients of the latter are mixed with
milk instead of water, and the finest flour
is made use of for them. Rolls require
only about twenty minutes for baking.

The life of a baker is very laborious ;

the greater part of his work is done by night : the journeyman is required always to commence his operations about eleven o'clock in the evening, in order to get the new bread ready for admitting the rolls in the morning. His wages are, however, but very moderate, seldom amounting to more than ten shillings a week, exclusive of his board.

The price of bread is regulated according to the price of wheat; and bakers are directed in this by the magistrates, whose rules they are bound to follow. By these the peck-loaf of each sort of bread must weigh seventeen pounds six ounces avoirdupois weight, and smaller loaves in the same proportion. Every sack of flour is to weigh two hundred and a half; and from this there ought to be made, at an average, twenty such peck-loaves, or eighty common quartern-loaves.

If bread were short in its weight only one ounce in thirty-six, the baker formerly was liable to be put in the pillory; and for the same offence he may now be fined, at the will of the magistrate, in any sum not less than one shilling, nor more than five shillings, for every ounce wanting; such bread being complained of and weighed in the presence of the magistrate within twenty-four hours after it is baked, because bread loses in weight by keeping.

The process of biscuit-baking, as practised at the Victualling-office at Deptford, is curious and interesting. The dough, which consists of flour and water only, is worked by a large machine. It is then handed over to a second workman, who slices it with a large knife for the bakers, of whom there are five. The first, or the *moulder*, forms the biscuits two at a time; the second, or *marker*, stamps and throws them to the splitter, who separates the two pieces, and puts them under the hand of the chucker, the man that supplies the oven, whose work of throwing the bread on the peel must be so exact, that he cannot look off for a moment. The fifth, or the depositer, receives the biscuits on the peel, and arranges them in the oven. All the men work with the greatest exactness, and are, in truth, like parts of the same machine. The business is to deposit in the oven seventy biscuits in a minute ; and this is accomplished with the regularity of a clock, the clacking of the peel operating like the motion of the pendulum. There are 12 ovens at Deptford, and each will furnish daily bread for 2040 men.

By referring to the plate, we see the baker represented in the act of kneading his dough : the bin upon which he is at work contains the flour: on his right hand is the peel, with which he puts in and takes out the bread : at his back we see the representation of the fire in the oven, and in the front is the pail in which the yeast is fetched daily from the brewhouse ; and by the side of the flour-bin on the ground is the wood used to heat the oven.

THE STRAW-HAT-MAKER.

THERE are few manufactures in the kingdom in which so little capital is wanted, or the knowledge of the art so soon acquired, as in that of straw-platting. One guinea is quite sufficient for the purchase of the machines and materials for employing 100 persons for several months.

The straw-hat-maker, represented in the plate, is employed in the making up of hats only, after the straw is braided or platted.

The straw is cut at the joints; and the outer covering being removed, it is sorted of equal sizes, and made up into bundles of eight or ten inches in length, and a foot in circumference. They are then to be dipped in water, and shaken a little so as not to retain too much moisture; and then the bundles are to be placed on their edges, in a box which is sufficiently close to prevent the evaporation of smoke. In the middle of the box is an earthen dish containing brimstone broken in small pieces: this is set on fire, and the box covered over and kept in the open air several hours.

It will be the business of one person to split and select the straws for 50

Straw Hat Maker. W. sc.

others who are braiders.   The splitting
is done by a small machine made principally of wood.   The straws, when
split, are termed splints, of which each
worker has a certain quantity : on one
end is wrapped a linen cloth, and they
are held under the arm and drawn out
as wanted.

Platters should be taught to use their
second fingers and thumbs, instead of
the forefingers, which are often required
to assist in turning the splints, and very
much facilitate the platting ; and they
should be cautioned against wetting the
splints too much.   Each platter should
have a small linen work-bag, and a
piece of pasteboard to roll the plat
round.   After five yards have been
worked up, it should be wound about
a piece of board half a yard wide,
fastened at the top with yarn, and
kept there several days to form it in a

proper shape. Four of these parcels, or a score, is the measurement by which the plat is sold.

A good platter can make three score a week, and good work will always command a sale both in winter and summer. The machines are small; they may be bought for two shillings each, and will last for many years.

When the straw is platted it comes into the hand of the person represented in the plate, who sews it together into hats, bonnets, &c. of various sizes and shapes, according to the prevailing fashions. They are then put on wooden blocks for the purpose of hot-pressing; and to render them of a more delicate white, they are again exposed to the fumes of sulphur.

Persons who make up these hats will earn half-a-guinea a week; but braiders, or platters, if very expert, will earn much more.

THE SOAP-BOILER.

THERE is scarcely any substance manufactured by the art of man more useful than that of soap ; and at first sight it may seem strange, that the article which is used to clean and whiten other substances should itself be formed of grease or oil, and that the coarsest of fat may be made into soap.

Soap is either hard or soft ; it is variously named according to its colour : thus we have white soap, mottled soap, yellow soap, &c. But all kinds are made with fat or oil, combined with quick-lime and potash, or soda.

Quick lime is a substance well-known ; *potash* is a salt obtained from vegetables in the following manner :—Vegetable substances, of any kind, burnt in the open air, and reduced to ashes, contain a certain proportion of salt, which is gained from the ashes by mixing them with water: and when the water is filtered, it is to be evaporated by heat, and the saline substance is left at the bottom of the vessel. This substance is called *potash*. *Soda* is obtained in the same way from the ashes of marine plants. Both potash and soda are called fixed *alkalis;* the *former* is denominated a *vegetable* alkali, the *latter* a *mineral* alkali.

The combination of soda, or potash, with oils or fat, forms soap; the union with *potash* affords *soft* soap, and the combination of *soda* with the same substances produces *hard* soap.

The formation of *white* soap may be shown on a small scale, b the following simple process:—Take by weight one part of lime, previously slaked, and two of soda; let them be boiled in

Soap Boiler.

W. R. sc.

twelve parts of water for half an hour, and then filter the fluid through a linen cloth till it is very clear. It must now be evaporated till a phial that would contain an ounce of water will hold an ounce and six drachms of the fluid. It is now called the *ley*. Mix one part of this ley with two parts of olive-oil in a glass or stone-ware vessel, and let it be beat up with a wooden spatula, and it soon becomes a consistent substance, and if left to stand four or five days it forms a white hard soap.

In large manufactories, such as that represented in the plate, the *ley* is made no stronger than to be able to sustain a new-laid egg; the workmen then begin to form the mixture. The oil or tallow is first boiled with a part of the *ley*, which may be diluted with water, till the whole is formed into a soapy compound. The stronger *ley* is then to be added, and kept slowly boiling, while a person, as is represented in the upper part of the plate, assists the union by constant agitation. When it is sufficiently boiled, a separation will appear to be taking place, the soap being at the top and the fluid below : to effect this separation completely, a quantity of common salt is added. The materials are usually boiled three or four hours ; when the fire is withdrawn. The soap is found united at the top of the liquor, which is now called the *waste ley*, and being of no further use it is drawn off.

The soap is now melted for the last time with another ley, or with water ; and when a little boiled it is cast into wooden frames, such as those represented in the plate. These frames are moveable, and range exactly one upon another, and the soap is filled in from the bottom to the top. When it is perfectly set and cold, the workman takes off the upper frame, and with a piece of copper wire he cuts off the soap which that frame contained. In this part of the business the man on the floor, in the plate, is represented as engaged. He then takes off another frame and so on till he come to within five or six of the bottom, and there he finds they *ley* has drained from the soap into the middle of the substance; of course, from this height to the bottom, the cakes of soap have an oval hole left in them. This ley he takes carefully out with an iron ladle, and puts it into the bucket that stands before him. By a like process he cuts the soap into narrow slices, as it is usually sold in the shops.

In France they make a cheap soap by using woollen rags, old woollen cloths, and even the horns of animals, &c. instead of oil. These substances are all soluble in caustic ley, and by proper boiling form a soap; but it has a very disagreeable smell.

The tallow for making soap is reckoned very good if 13 cwt. of it, with alkali, will yield a ton weight of soap.

Yellow soap is made with tallow and resin, in the proportion of ten parts of tallow to three and a half of resin; and these, if good, will, with alkali, yield twenty of soap.

Mottled soap obtains its speckled appearance by dispersing the ley, towards the end of the operation, through the soap, or by adding to it a quantity of sulphate of iron, which, by its decomposition, deposits its oxide through the soap, and gives it the appearance of streaked marble. Some manufacturers use the oxide of manganese for the same purpose.

Soap is easily and completely dissolved in soft water, but in hard water it curdles, or is only imperfectly dissolved: on this account a solution of soap in spirits of wine is used to discover whether water of any spring or pond be soft or hard; for if the water be soft the solution will unite with it, but if it be hard the soap will separate in flakes.

The soap-manufacturer is subject to the excise laws, and he pays a heavy duty for every pound of soap that he makes. His coppers, and even furnace-doors, are furnished with locks and keys, and he dares not open them but in the presence of an excise-officer, and he must give notice of twenty-four hours or more, in writing, to the officers before he begins a making. His house is no longer an Englishman's castle, into which none may come but by his leave: the excise-officers are required to enter it at all times, by day and by night; who may, between the hours of five in the morning and eleven at night, unlock and examine every copper, and every part of the dwelling-house, none daring to obstruct them without incurring very heavy penalties. To similar restrictions the tallow-chandler, and other trades under the excise laws, are subject.

———

THE PLUMBER.

THE business of the plumber consists in the art of casting and working of lead, and using it in buildings. He furnishes us with a cistern for water, and with a sink for the kitchen; he covers the house with lead, and makes the gutters to carry away the rain-water;

Plumber.

W.P. Sc.

he makes pipes of all sorts and sizes, and sometimes he casts leaden statues as ornaments for the garden. The plumber also is employed in making coffins for those who are to be interred out of the common way. And besides these departments in his trade, the modern plumber makes no small share of his profits by fitting up patent water-closets. Of these there are many different kinds, and but few inventions in modern days have answered so well to the patentees as these.

The chief articles in plumbery consisting in sheets and pipes of lead, we shall briefly describe the processes of making them.

In casting *sheet-lead* a sort of table, or mould, is used, about four or five feet wide, and sixteen or eighteen feet long; it must slope a little from the end in which the metal is poured on, and the

slope must be greater in proportion to
the thinness of the lead wanted.   The
mould is spread over with moistened
sand about two inches thick, and made
perfectly smooth by means of a piece
of wood called a *strike*.   At the upper
end of the mould is a pan of a triangular shape. The lead, being melted, is
put by means of ladles into this pan ;
and when it is cool enough, two men
take the pan by the handle, (or else one
of them lifts it by a bar and chain fixed
to the beam in the ceiling,) and pour it
into the mould, while another man
stands ready with the *strike* to sweep
the lead forward, and draw the over-
plus into a trough ready to receive it.
The sheets being thus cast, it remains
only to roll them up or cut them to any
particular size.

If a cistern is wanted, they measure
out the four sides, and form any figures

intended to be raised on the front in the sand, and cast as before; the sides are then soldered together, after which the bottom is soldered in.

Pipes are cast in a kind of mill, with arms or levers to turn it. The moulds are of hollow brass, consisting of two pieces, about two feet and a half long, which open and shut by means of hinges and hooks. In the middle of these moulds is placed a core or round solid piece of brass or iron, somewhat longer than the mould. This core is passed through two copper rundles, one at each end of the mould, which they serve to close; to these is joined a little copper tube two inches long, and of the thickness of the intended leaden pipe. These tubes retain the core exactly in the middle of the cavity of the mould, and then the lead is poured in through an aperture in the shape of a funnel. When the mould is full, a hook is put into the core, and, turning the mill, it is drawn out, and the pipe is made. If it is to be lengthened, they put one end of it in the lower end of the mould, and the end of the core into it, then shut the mould again, and apply its rundle and tube as before, the pipe just cast serving for a rundle, &c. at the other end. Metal is again poured in which unites with the other pipe, and so the operation is repeated till the pipe is of the length required.

Large pipes of sheet-lead are made by wrapping the lead on wooden cylinders of the proper length, and then soldering it up the edges.

In this country it is not unfrequent that the business of glazier, plumber, and painter, is united under the same person; but the plumbing trade is of itself, in London, reckoned a very good one for the master. The health of the men is often injured by the fumes of the lead. Journeymen earn about thirty shillings a week; and we recommend earnestly to lads brought up to either of the beforementioned trades, that they cultivate cleanliness and strict sobriety, and that they never, on any account, eat their meals, or retire to rest at night, before they have well washed their hands and face.

THE DYER.

THE art of the dyer consists in tinge-ing cloth, stuff, or other substance, with a permanent colour which penetrates the substance of it. Dyeing differs from bleaching, which is not the giving a new colour but the brightening an old one. It differs also from painting, printing, or stamping, because the colours in these only reach the surface. The nature of the dyer's business is very well represented in the opposite plate.

The mystery of the art of dyeing consists chiefly in chemical processes, and it comprises a vast collection of chemical experiments. The substances principally subjected to this art are wool, hair, silk, cotton, hemp, and flax. Of these, the animal productions, namely, wool, hair, and silk, take the dye more readily than the vegetable substances, cotton, hemp, and flax, because they seem to have a stronger attraction for the colouring particles of the various dyes employed.

Wool is naturally of a greasy nature, and requires to be scoured before it is submitted to the process of dyeing.

Silk, previously to dyeing, must be washed with soap and warm water, and then in a cold solution of alum and water.

Cottons and *linens* require bleaching, and scouring in an alkaline ley. They must then be washed in a solution of alum and water, and afterwards in a decoction of galls, or some other astringent, as hot as the operator can bear it.

The first step in dyeing is the application of what is termed a *mordant ;* that is, something must be employed to make the substances take the dye ; for by merely immersing them into the dyeing liquor they will seldom take or retain a deep dye.

Different mordants are used for preparing different goods, and for preparing the same goods for different colouring drugs. Alum is the most extensively useful, being always employed in the case of linens and cottons. For the dyeing of silk and wool, metallic solutions are more frequently employed as mordants, because these have a stronger

stronger attraction for animal than for vegetable substances.

In dyeing there are but three simple colours, the *red*, *yellow*, and *blue*; all other colours are compounded of these. Different shades or tints of the same colour are produced by using different drugs, or by varying the quantity of colouring particles.

Cochineal, kermes, and gum-lac, among the animal productions, and madder, archil, carthamus, and Brazil wood, among the vegetables, are the chief substances employed as *red* dyes.

All the substances employed for dyeing *yellow* colours are vegetable productions; and the principal *blue* dyes are from indigo, woad, logwood, and Prussian blue.

Compound colours are produced sometimes by mixing the simple colours in the dyeing liquor, and sometimes by

A Dyer.   W. So.

A Potter.

VH.sc.

dyeing the stuff first in a bath of one simple colour, then in another.

In London there are dyers of all sorts ; some dye only wool, others silk ; some confine themselves to particular colours, such as scarlet and blues. The scarlet dyer is said to be the most ingenious and most profitable. The business of a dyer of woollens is laborious and chilly, the workmen are constantly dabbling in water hot and cold. Silk-dyers have the least laborious business ; journeymen will easily earn thirty shillings a week.

——

THE POTTER.

Pottery, or the art of making vessels of baked earth, is of very remote antiquity. The antient Greeks and Etruscans particularly excelled in it.

Porcelain, the most perfect speces of pottery, has been made in China from time immemorial.

Clay and flints are substances of which every kind of earthen-ware is made: clay alone shrinks and cracks, the flint gives it solidity and strength.

The wheel and the lathe are the chief instruments in the business of pottery: the first is intended for large works, and the other for small ; the wheel is turned by a labourer, as is represented in the plate, but the lathe is put into motion by the foot of the workman.

When the clay is properly prepared, and made into lumps proportioned to the size of the cup, plate, or other vessel to be made, the potter places one of these lumps upon the head of the wheel before him, which he turns round, while he forms the cavity of the vessel with his finger and thumb, continuing to

widen it from the middle, and thus turning the inside into form with one hand,
while he proportions the outside with
the other, the wheel being kept the
whole time in constant motion. The
mouldings are formed by holding a piece
of wood or iron, cut into the shape of
the moulding, to the vessel while the
wheel is going round ; but the feet and
handles are made by themselves, and set
on by the hand ; and if there be any
sculpture in the work, it is usually made
in wooden moulds, and struck on piece
by piece on the outside of the vessel.
When the vessel is finished, the workman cuts it off from the remaining part
of the clay, and sets it aside to dry ; and
when it is hardened sufficiently to bear
removing without danger, it is covered
with a glazing made of a composition of
lead and put into a furnace, where it is
baked. Some sorts are glazed by throw-

ing sea-salt into the furnace among the different pieces of pottery. The salt is decomposed, and the vapours of it form a glazing upon the vessels: this is not, however, a good glazing.

English stone-ware is made of tobacco-pipe clay, mixed with flints calcined and ground. This mixture burns white, and vessels of this kind were formerly all glazed with sea-salt. Wedgewood's *queen's ware* is made of tobacco-pipe clay, much beaten in water. By this process the finer parts of the clay remain suspended in the water, while the coarser and all impurities fall to the bottom. The thick liquid is further purified by passing it through hair and lawn sieves, after which it is mixed with another liquid, consisting of flints calcined, ground, and suspended in water. The mixture is then dried in a kiln; and being afterwards beaten to a proper temper, it be-

comes fit for being formed at the wheel
into dishes, plates, bowls, &c.

When this ware is to be put into the
furnace to be baked, the several pieces
of it are placed in cases made of clay,
which are piled one upon another in the
dome of the furnace; a fire is then
lighted, and the ware is brought into a
proper temper for glazing. By being
baked, the ware acquires a strong pro-
perty of imbibing moisture; in this state
it is called *biscuit;* and when dipped
into the glaze, consisting of water made
thick with white lead and ground flints,
it attracts it into its pores, and the ware
presently becomes dry. It is then exposed a second time to the fire, and a
thin glossy coat is formed on the surface.
The colour of the coat is more or less
yellow according as a greater or less proportion of lead has been used. The lead
is principally instrumental in producing

the glaze, as well as giving it the yellow colour ; the flint serves only to give a consistency to the lead during the time of its vitrification.

———

THE TYPE-FOUNDER.

THE first part of the type-founder's business is to prepare the metal, which is a composition of lead and regulus of antimony, melted together in a furnace. In large founderies this metal is cast into bars of twenty pounds each, which are delivered to the workmen as occasions may require ; this is a laborious and un-wholesome part of the business, owing to the fumes which are thrown off. Fif-teen hundred weight of this metal is cast in a day, and the founders usually cast as much at one casting as will last six months.

Type Founder. WR. *sc.*

We now come to the letter-cutter; that is, to him who cuts the moulds in which the letters are cast; and he must be provided with vices, hammers, files, gravers, and gauges of various kinds. He then prepares steel punches, on the face of which he draws or marks the exact shape of the letter, and with pointed gravers and sculpters he digs out the steel between the strokes or marks which he made on the face of the punch, leaving the marks standing. Having shaped the inside strokes of the letter, he deepens the hollows with the same tools; for, if a letter be not deep in proportion to its width, it will, when used at press, print black, and be good for nothing. He then works the outside with files till it is fit for the matrice.

A matrice is a piece of brass or copper about an inch and half long, and

thick in proportion to the size of the
letter it is to contain. In this metal
is sunk the face of the letter intended
to be cast, by striking the letter-punch.
After this the sides and face of the matrice must be cleared, with files, of all
bunchings made by sinking the punch.

When the metal and other things are
properly prepared, the matrice is fastened to the end of the mould, which
the caster holds in his left hand, while
he pours the metal in with his right;
by a sudden jerk of the hand the metal
runs into the cavity of the matrice and
takes the figure or impression. The
mould consists of an under and an upper half, of which the latter is taken
off as soon as the letter is cast, and the
caster throws the letter upon a sheet of
paper, laid for the purpose on a bench
or table, and he is then ready to cast
another letter as before.

When the casters have made a certain number of types, which are made
much longer than they are wanted,
boys come and break away the jets, or
extra lengths from the types; the jets
they cast into the pot, and the types
are carried to the man who is represented sitting at his work in the plate,
who polishes their broad sides. This
is a very dexterous operation; for the
man, in turning up the types, does it
so quickly, by a mere touch of the fingers of the left hand, as not to require
the least perceptible intermission in the
motion of the right hand upon the
stone.

The caster represented in the plate is
seen in the act of pouring the metal into the mould. He takes it up with a
small ladle from the pan, which is constantly kept over the fire in a sort of
stove under the brick-work. The iron

plate on the right hand of the the caster is to defend him from the heat of the
fire, and the screen between the two
workmen is to prevent the man sitting
from being injured by the metal, which
is apt to fly about by the operation of
casting. On the table near the newly
cast types, are several blocks of the
metal, with which the caster replenishes
his pan as he makes the letters.

A type-founder will cast upwards of
3000 letters in a day; and the perfection
of letters thus cast, consists in their being all strait and square; of the same
height, and evenly lined, without slop-
ing one way or the other.

What is called a fount or font of letter, is a quantity of each kind cast by the
letter-founder and properly sorted. A
complete font includes, besides the running letter, all the single letters, double
letters, points, commas, lines, borders,

head and tail pieces, and numerical characters.

Letter-founders have a kind of list by which they regulate their founts : this is absolutely necessary, as some letters are much more frequently used than others, of course the cells containing these should be better stored than those of the letters which do not so often recur. Thus a fount does not contain an equal number of *a* and *b*, or of *e* and *z*. In a fount containing a hundred thousand characters, the *a* should have five thousand, the *c* three thousand, the *e* eleven thousand, the *i* six thousand, and the other letters in proportion.

Printers order their founts either by the hundred weight or by the sheet. If they order a fount of five hundred they mean that the whole shall weigh about 500 lb. ; but if they demand a fount of ten sheets, it is understood,

that with this fount they shall be able
to compose ten sheets, or twenty forms,
without being obliged to distribute.
The founder reckons 120 lb. to a sheet,
but this varies with the nature of the
letter.